For Aidan, and his brilliant Snurtch
—S. F.

For Jen, thank you for putting up with my Snurtches
—C. S.

ATHENEUM BOOKS FOR YOUNG READERS
An imprint of Simon & Schuster Children's Publishing Division
1230 Avenue of the Americas, New York, New York 10020
Text copyright © 2016 by Sean Ferrell
Illustrations copyright © 2016 by Charles Santoso
All rights reserved, including the right of reproduction in whole or in part
in any form.
ATHENEUM BOOKS FOR YOUNG READERS is a registered trademark of
Simon & Schuster, Inc.
Atheneum logo is a trademark of Simon & Schuster, Inc.
For information about special discounts for bulk purchases, please
contact Simon & Schuster Special Sales at 1-866-506-1949 or
business@simonandschuster.com.
The Simon & Schuster Speakers Bureau can bring authors to your
live event. For more information or to book an event, contact the
Simon & Schuster Speakers Bureau at 1-866-248-3049 or visit our
website at www.simonspeakers.com.
Book design by Ann Bobco
The text for this book was set in 24HRS.
The illustrations for this book were rendered in pencil and colored
digitally.
Manufactured in China
0616 SCP
First Edition
10  9  8  7  6  5  4  3  2  1
Library of Congress Cataloging-in-Publication Data
Ferrell, Sean.
The Snurtch / words by Sean Ferrell ; pictures by Charles Santoso.—
First edition.
pages cm
Summary: "Ruthie has a problem at school. It is the Snurtch. The
Snurtch is a scribbly, grabby, rude monster who follows Ruthie around
and gets her into all sorts of trouble. It seems Ruthie will never be rid
of the Snurtch. But eventually, she realizes she's not the only one . . .
George has one too"—Provided by publisher.
ISBN 978-1-4814-5656-2 (hardcover)
ISBN 978-1-4814-5657-9 (eBook)
[1. Behavior—Fiction. 2. Imaginary playmates—Fiction.]
I. Santoso, Charles, illustrator. II. Title.
PZ7.1.F468Sn 2016
[E]—dc23    2015017875

# the Snurtch

words by Sean Ferrell

pictures by Charles Santoso

A
atheneum

ATHENEUM
Books for Young Readers

New York   London   Toronto   Sydney   New Delhi

Ruthie has a problem at school.

It is not the students.
It is not the classroom.

It is not the reading
or the writing
or the math.

It is the Snurtch.

Teacher says, "Ruthie, please take your seat."

There is her seat.

And there is the Snurtch.

The Snurtch is lots of things. Nice is not one of them.

The Snurtch
is scribbly and
scrunchy.

The Snurtch is grabby
and burpy and rude.

And the Snurtch is
always with Ruthie.

When Teacher calls on Ruthie, the Snurtch throws her pencils.
And Ruthie forgets the question.

During recess the Snurtch makes rude noises,
and no one wants Ruthie to play.

And when everyone draws in art class, the Snurtch becomes truly terrible.

It hides.

It waits.

And when Teacher asks if anyone wants to share their work . . .

it leaps.
     It grabs.
          It crumples.
               It makes sure no one will like George's drawing.

Teacher says, "Ruthie, that is NOT okay."

"It wasn't me," says Ruthie.
"It was the Snurtch."

No one has a life as difficult as Ruthie's.

Ten whole minutes later, Ruthie tries to draw something pretty.
Or cute. Or happy. But all that comes out of her crayon is
unhappy scribbles.

The Snurtch is no help.

Ruthie looks really hard at the Snurtch.

Ruthie draws.

Art class ends.

Teacher asks if anyone would like to share.

No one is more surprised than Ruthie when she stands up.
No one except the Snurtch.

"I will," says Ruthie.

She shows the class her drawing.
Her classmates look.

"It's what throws our pencils," says one.
"It's what makes weird noises," says another.

"It's what drew on my drawing," says George.

Ruthie knows the Snurtch wants to run away and hide.
"I'm sorry about that," says Ruthie.
"That's okay," says George. "And I like your drawing."

And then another
kid says the same.
And another and
another, until
everyone agrees . . .

Ruthie has drawn a wonderful Snurtch.

Ruthie likes school.
She likes the students.
She likes the classroom.
She likes the reading and the writing and the math.

And Ruthie still has a Snurtch.

The Snurtch
is still scribbly
and scrunchy.

The Snurtch
is still burpy and
grabby and rude.

But the Snurtch also listens sometimes.

And sometimes the Snurtch is even sorry.

And as hard as it can be to sit next to a Snurtch,
Ruthie realizes she's not alone.

George has one too.

"Thanks,"
says George.

"I like your
drawing,"
says Ruthie.